Shnook
the Peddler

Shnook
the Peddler

by Maxine Schur

Illustrated by Dale Redpath

GEMSTONE BOOKS

Dillon Press, Inc.   Minneapolis, Minnesota 55415

Library of Congress Cataloging in Publication Data

Schur, Maxine.
  Shnook the peddler.

  "Gemstone books."
  Summary: A young boy in turn-of-the-century rural Russia
learns that appearances are often deceiving after he steals and
then tries to return a dreidel to the traveling peddler Shnook.
  1. Children's stories, American. [1. Peddlers and
peddling—Fiction.   2. Jews—Soviet Union—Fiction]
I. Redpath, Dale, ill.   II. Title.
PZ7.S3964Sh   1985   [Fic]   85-6807
ISBN 0-87518-298-4

Dillon Press, Inc., 242 Portland Avenue South
Minneapolis, Minnesota 55415

Printed in the United States of America
1 2 3 4 5 6 7 8 9 10 93 92 91 90 89 88 87 86 85

For Aaron

Shnook
the Peddler

In Korovenko, late summer was always hot and damp. The rye grew as high as corn, the air smelled of fallen plums, and near our thatched roof hut the river babbled all day like a happy child.

But in all this warm beauty there was little time for play. From sunrise to sunset there was heder, and after that, supper, prayers, and bed. On Shabbos we rested, studied the Talmud, and strolled through the plum orchards on the other side of the village. Only on Wednesday when heder let out two hours early did we boys get a chance to run, yell, play Cossacks, and swish our bare feet into the tickle-cold waters of the river.

One Wednesday afternoon as we were making wooden swords from oak branches that had fallen to the ground, my best friend, Moshe, asked me, "Leibush, have you seen Shnook the Peddler?"

"What? Is Shnook back in town?"

"Sure. He arrived last night and slept in the synagogue. Dovid saw his wagon there this morning."

"Maybe he'll come to our house again!" I yelled jumping up. "Maybe he's there now!"

Grabbing my sword, I ran up the riverbank toward home. Any peddler who happened through our poor village brought enough excitement to last until Shevuos. Shnook, however, was crazier than any of them, and I especially didn't want to miss the show!

Lucky me. There at the side of our hut was his broken down cart and his old nag, Fresser, scaring our chickens into high-pitched shrieking.

I opened the door and saw my father and Shnook

sitting at our table, drinking glasses of tea. Standing between them, my mother cut two large slices of her honey cake. Shnook chewed the cake slowly. He was not old, but his face was thin and dry, and his hands were bony and rough from driving his cart. His smile was warm, and yet he spoke so little, my father once said his words must be weighed, not counted. Shimon was his real name, but because he was so strange, the children of Korovenko called him Shnook.

Now Shnook stood up and in his meek voice said, "Please come and see what I have." As I edged closer, Shnook suddenly looked at me and then smiled at my father. "Your boy has gotten bigger," he said.

"Yes," Papa beamed. "In summer Leibush grows like a wildflower."

Shnook smiled at me for several moments. Even though I was sure that he must be a fool, I smiled

back. No one puzzled me more than Shnook the Peddler. I was curious about him because he was so different than anyone I had seen. Moshe and I would whisper after each of his visits, "Shnook the Peddler is *meshuga*! Crazy!"

Some of the older boys, Dovid and Kalmen, said he was bad. They believed he had been put under a spell by the Evil Eye, and that's why he bungled things. They said he had magic powers and could use certain words to trick you, make you forget your name, and cause feathers to sprout from your ears and onions to grow in your navel.

I didn't know what to believe. Papa had many times warned me about speaking against people. He told me what I didn't see with my eyes not to make up with my mouth. And yet surely Shnook was cut from a different cloth than the other peddlers who traveled through the village. Other peddlers opened their shiny traveling bags, waved their arms, and smiled like fathers at a wedding as they talked about their goods.

"Good Jewish wife, allow me please to show to you the most wonderful of stewpots! For your scrupulous inspection, I have here straight from St. Petersburg, a silver-toned pot fit for a fat goose at the table of the Czar, may a thunderbolt find his head!"

After noisy bargaining back and forth, other peddlers would stay for a glass of tea and then another, a cookie, a slice of honey cake, and, more often than not, a supper of soup and groats. The whole world lay on their tongues, and when the oil lamps burned low, these peddlers who drove from Vitebsk to Chichelnik wove stories of the Czar's court. They brought the news from St. Petersburg, Vladivostok, and Odessa. They described the fashions of the cities to the delight of the women, all the while pinching the cheeks of the children and slipping candies into their small hands.

But Shnook was different.

The villagers said that if Shnook sold coffins, people would stop dying. The truth was nothing he did turned out right. One time he left his goods at home and traveled to Khotin with an empty bag. Another time he left his bag open near a kitchen door where a goat was tied up. The goat ate five pairs of socks and a hat. Still another time he sold everything in his bag to himself and gave the items as presents to a poor family.

There's a saying: "When a foolish buyer goes to market, the sellers rejoice." But in Korovenko when Shnook the Peddler arrived, the buyers rejoiced! Shnook had no idea of sales talk. If someone showed interest in his goods, he would often shake his head and explain, "No? You really want to buy those handkerchiefs? The cloth is thin and rough. Better you should keep your money." Even stranger, Shnook had no idea how to buy goods, so he would often end up with such odd things even he did not know what they were. Once he tried to sell spatulas as shoe horns, and another time he bought three hundred fountain pens—all of them leaking. "He has such bad luck," people joked, "even his fountain pens cry!"

Other peddlers didn't like the villagers to touch their goods. They tapped their feet and chattered so much no one had a chance of getting close to their things. But not Shnook.

Now as my mother and father watched, Shnook opened his ragged leather bag. He took his goods out so silently you would have thought he was hiding them rather than presenting them for sale.

Onto the flax mat that covered our dirt floor, Shnook carefully laid red silk ribbons, woolen shawls, sheets of writing paper, matches, children's shoes, eyeglasses, bottles of rosewater, embroidered pillowcases, featherbed covers, wooden spoons, jars of ink, boot polish, satin covered buttons, boot hooks, tin scissors, tiny wood boxes of needles, bone combs, thimbles, and lace tablecloths—handmade in Poland.

When Shnook came to the religious items, he showed special care. On the table he gently placed hallah bread covers, prayer shawls, shabbos candles, and my favorite, the four-sided Hanukkah tops we called dreidels. These were fist-sized dreidels, hand carved from birch wood, that could spin nearly three minutes without falling!

We stared wide-eyed at all the beautiful new things from faraway places. In a moment Shnook had changed our soot-stained hut into a colorful market fair. Even Papa, who took little notice of such things, looked amazed. Shnook stood back and stared down at his boots as if discovering two old friends. He always seemed shy when showing his goods and so waited for my mother to make the first move.

My mother, never wishing to cause him discomfort, began to look over the goods very carefully, one by one. I watched the way my mother gently touched the heavy cotton cloth from Zhitomir. It was deep blue, the color of cornflowers, and I knew my mother wished to buy it. To sew it, to dress me up like a heder boy from Vitebsk. But we were not for that sort of thing. My trousers were made from Papa's old ones. My shirt was cut from Mama's old dress. Even my jacket had once been Uncle Solly's coat.

Mama never had more than one ruble to spend, and this time she chose soap, matches, and shabbos candles. When she picked out what she wanted, she asked how much they cost, and the magic was that Shnook the Peddler always said, "One ruble."

Mama sighed and handed Shnook the ruble. As he wrote out the list of goods my mother had bought, I noticed one of the dreidels had fallen off the table and lay under the chair. The peddler picked his goods off the table and put them back into his bag, but he did not see the fallen dreidel. I should have picked it up and handed it to him, but something inside me froze.

As he gathered his things, I stood in front of the chair so he could not see the dreidel and reasoned frantically. *He won't miss it; after all, he never notices anything! Besides, I'll just borrow it, and the next time he comes around I'll find a way to slip it back to him. No harm will be done to anybody.*

Just then my father's voice interrupted my thoughts.
"Shimon, the sky is dark now, and the air is heavy.
We would be honored if you would share our supper
with us and stay the night."

As always, Shnook made some excuse to go. "Thank
you, but Dubne is still two days away, and I want
to get there by Shabbos." Then he picked up his
heavy bag and heaved it onto his shoulder.

"Shimon," my mother said softly, "where will
you go if it rains?"

The peddler opened the door. "This is my home.
My carpet is the road, my ceiling the sky, and my
lamps the stars." Then he was gone.

That night after prayers, I climbed on my bed
above the warm brick oven and listened to the
crashing sound of the late summer storm. I had
hidden the dreidel under my feather bed, and now
I took it out to feel its smooth wood in the dark.

My parents fell asleep quickly, but I could not sleep. They say a thief has an easy job but difficult dreams. I tossed from side to side, more unhappy than I'd ever been before. My mind spun like a dreidel as I imagined being in jail, laughed at, teased, and hated. "There is Leibush, the thief, the thief." I saw my father, my mother, the rabbi, my teacher, all pointing their fingers at me while the stolen dreidel burned in my hand. I wanted to cry, but I couldn't.

Outside the rain pounded down as if it were crying for me, and all the while scary pictures stormed through my mind. When the nightmare faded, I could still see the trusting face of Shnook. Suddenly I understood clearly that I had done wrong. I had tried to trick someone who was kind and gentle. I knew I had to change what I had done.

I hooked up my boots in the dark and slipped

the dreidel into my coat pocket. Praying that I would be strong enough to meet the peddler, I very slowly opened the door and slipped out into the rain.

I ran through the village, heading for the synagogue. I hoped if Shnook would be in any dry place tonight, he would be there. The night was wild. In the black sky, long ghostly clouds traveled quickly across the heavens. The wind howled like a dog in pain, and the rain beat down upon the twisted cobblestone streets.

Reaching the synagogue, I went to the door and found it slightly open. I had straight in my mind what I was going to say to him. I would confess my mistake right away and give back the dreidel. Then I would ask him to forgive me.

I trembled as I entered the synagogue, partly from the cold but mostly from fear. Inside, the oil lamps burned brightly. As I walked in, the rain dripped off me, forming small puddles on the floor. Just then, I heard loud, beautiful singing—in a voice so strong and powerful for a moment I couldn't move. Shnook the Peddler was not here. Someone else, some strong-voiced traveler, had most likely come into the synagogue to get out of the rain. I was so disappointed I began to cry.

The man broke off his beautiful song and walked toward me. His face was so bright with happiness that at first I did not recognize Shnook the Peddler.

"Leibush!" he said. "What are you doing here on this terrible night?"

His words startled me, and for a few horrible seconds I had forgotten why I was there and could do nothing but cry. At last my tears stopped, and I said through chattering teeth, "I came to bring you this. You left it in our home. I mean . . . I stole it." Slowly, I pulled the dreidel from my pocket.

The tears came again. Shnook pulled a handker-chief from his pocket and dried my face. This made me feel babyish yet somehow good, too.

"Come," he said, pulling dry clothes from his bag in the corner. "Change your clothes."

When I had changed, the storm still raged, so Shnook insisted I remain in the synagogue and sleep on his feather bed.

As we bedded down I said, "I'm sorry I took your dreidel."

Shnook quietly replied, "I know you are."

"But why aren't you angry with me?" I asked.

He looked at me for a few seconds, smoothing his beard. "First of all," he said with his shy smile, "I knew you had taken it."

"You knew! You knew all along?"

"I saw you put it in your pocket. Thank the Lord you are not a good thief!"

"You knew...and still you're not angry! Why aren't you angry?" For some reason my own voice had anger in it.

"We are both in the Lord's house. We do not need to be angry here. You were angry at yourself. That's what really mattered."

Shnook the Peddler wrapped himself in his coat and covered me with his feather bed. His coat was too short to cover his feet, and I saw his socks filled with holes. We went to sleep.

When we woke, the synagogue was still dark. After dressing and praying, Shnook hitched Fresser to his cart and said good-bye. In that gray silent world that comes before dawn, I watched him steer his old cart down the mud-washed road toward Dubne.

I turned towards home. My sleeping village lay cold and wet around me, giving off the odor of damp wood and musty hay. I reached home before

my parents woke and slipped silently back into bed.

Though he came back to Korovenko for many years, I never again called him Shnook the Peddler. He was Shimon the Peddler, the good, the strong, the kind. He was the man who left cotton, the color of cornflowers, by our door, and on Hanukkah, a big, birch-carved dreidel. I have it to this day.

Every year on snowy Hanukkah nights when the candles burn short and in the holiday joy the dreidel spins its lone path across our floor, I can still see him traveling to Dubne, his carpet the road, his ceiling the sky, and his lamps the stars.

Word of Explanation

Shnook the Peddler takes place in a small village in Russia just before the turn of the twentieth century. Leibush and his family and friends as well as Shnook are Russian Jews, and, therefore, some of the vocabulary found in the story is Jewish as well as Russian in origin.

The Jewish terms, the names of religious items and holidays, come from either the Hebrew or Yiddish language. The language of the Jews in Russia was Yiddish, a mixture of German and Hebrew. Hebrew, the language of the Jewish religion, was used in prayer. The list of words on the following page gives the origin of each word as well as the definition.

Glossary

Cossacks (Russian)—a group of frontiersmen from southern Russia, who rode as part of the army of the czar

czar (Russian)—the name given to the ruler of Russia until the revolution in 1917, which overthrew the czarist government

dreidel (Yiddish)—a four-sided Hanukkah top, each side decorated with a Hebrew letter

hallah (Hebrew)—a white braided bread used on the Sabbath and holidays

Hanukkah (Hebrew)—an eight-day Jewish holiday also known as the Festival of Lights. It usually occurs in December

heder (Hebrew)—a Jewish religious elementary school

meshuga (Hebrew)—crazy

ruble (Russian)—the basic unit of money in Russia, which would be comparable to dollars in American money

Shabbos (Hebrew)—the Jewish Sabbath

Shevuos (Hebrew)—a late spring harvest festival

synagogue (Greek)—the Jewish place of worship

Talmud (Hebrew)—a collection of Jewish religious and civil laws

About the Author

As versatile as the goods of her
character, Shnook, Maxine Schur
has done a variety of exciting work.
Graduating from the University of
California at Berkeley with a degree
in theatre arts, she has worked in
New Zealand as a film editor, actress,
and writer. Her first two children's
books were published in New Zealand.

In California, her present home,
Ms. Schur has worked as a children's
book columnist. She also co-founded
a professional writing service and
presently designs educational software.
Maxine Schur currently resides in San
Mateo with her husband and two
children.